ALADDIN AND HIS WONDERFUL LAMP

One day, while walking through the wood, Aladdin saw a man kneeling in front of a tree which had a large hole in its trunk. When the man saw Aladdin coming, he said to him, "If you go inside this hole and bring me the lamp you find at the bottom, you can take anything you like."

Aladdin went down into the trunk of the tree and saw marvellous treasures.

"Take what treasures you like. Bring me only the lamp," said the man from above. But Aladdin, suspecting that the man was a magician and the lamp was very valuable, refused to come out.

Then, the magician became very angry and left him shut inside the tree-trunk.

Aladdin, seeing no hope of rescue, unintentionally rubbed the lamp. Instantly, there appeared a genie who said to him, "Master, what is your will ?" Aladdin, very surprised, asked him to release him from the tree-trunk.

Immediately, Aladdin found himself back at home. He presented his mother with a tray filled with delicious fruit.

"Look mother ! I have brought a magic lamp for you. From now onwards, we shall want for nothing, for I have found a wonderful lamp in which lives a genie who can do anything," said Aladdin to his mother.

"How lovely my son ! If it is so, we shall be able to give a present to our King who is so kind to all his people," said Aladdin's mother.

When Aladdin presented rich gifts to the King the next day, he saw the Princess whose matchless beauty persuaded Aladdin to ask the King for her hand in marriage.

"You can marry her, if you get a marble palace built in a single night as a wedding gift for the Princess," replied the King.

Aladdin got the palace built at the appointed place and married the Princess with the help of the genie. They lived very happily. One day, the wicked magician, hearing of the good luck of Aladdin and knowing he was away, took advantage of his absence to present himself at the palace.

He tricked the Princess by exchanging the wonderful lamp for a new one. As soon as he had the genie in his power, the magician ordered him to carry the palace far away to another land.

When Aladdin returned, he learnt what had happened. He sat up on the magic carpet he had found in the enchanted tree and went in pursuit of the magician. He caught the wicked magician and killed him then and there. Then, he returned to his country with the pretty Princess, the wonderful lamp and the marble palace. Both Aladdin and the Princess lived happily ever after.

THE ELVES AND THE SHOEMAKER

Once upon a time, there was a shoemaker. He was so poor that he could not afford to buy even leather to make shoes with.

He would often go to sleep on an empty stomach. But he was hopeful of good luck.

When he woke up one morning, he was dumb-founded by what he saw. To his surprise, there was a lovely pair of shoes lying on the floor. 'Who have put them here ?' said the shoemaker to himself.

After some time, a customer arrived at his workshop. When the customer saw that lovely pair of shoes, he paid the shoemaker good money.

"Congratulations, my good man ! These are the best and most beautiful shoes I have ever seen," said the customer to the shoemaker, "My daughter will be pleased when I give them to her as her birthday-gift."

The next day, the shoemaker found another pair of shoes.

'How lovely these shoes ! I shall never be poor again. Who have put them here ?' the shoemaker wondered.

That night, the shoemaker hid himself in his workshop to know of the reality.

At midnight, he saw some elves enter the workshop through an open window.

As soon as they entered, they set about the business of making the shoes. 'I see. They have been helping me. They are wearing few clothes in this winter. I should also help them by giving them clothes,' said the shoemaker.

The shoemaker went to town. He bought plenty of clothes to give to the little elves to show his gratitude for the good deeds they had done.

At midnight, the little elves arrived at the shoemaker's workshop. They felt very pleased when they saw the lovely presents.

They unwrapped the presents and found the clothes which were meant for them.

From that day on, the shoemaker never lacked money to buy leather. He lived the rest of his life in prosperity.

KING MIDAS

There was a miserly King named Midas. He was ambitious. His aim in life was to amass more and more gold. He paid no attention to the needs of his subjects.

17

He was not satisfied with the gold he had amassed. One day, he called upon a famous magician.

"I want you to use your magic to make my treasures multiply," the King said to the magician.

"I shall give you such an extraordinary power in your hands that no living person on this Earth will ever have," said the magician to the King, "Hold out your hands."

The magician gently tapped the hands of the King and said, "From now onwards, everything you touch will turn into gold."

As a result, whatever thing the King touched was transformed into the purest gold.

To his utter surprise, when he went to eat, all the food he touched was also changed into gold.

The King was not, at all, pleased. He thought that he would starve to death.

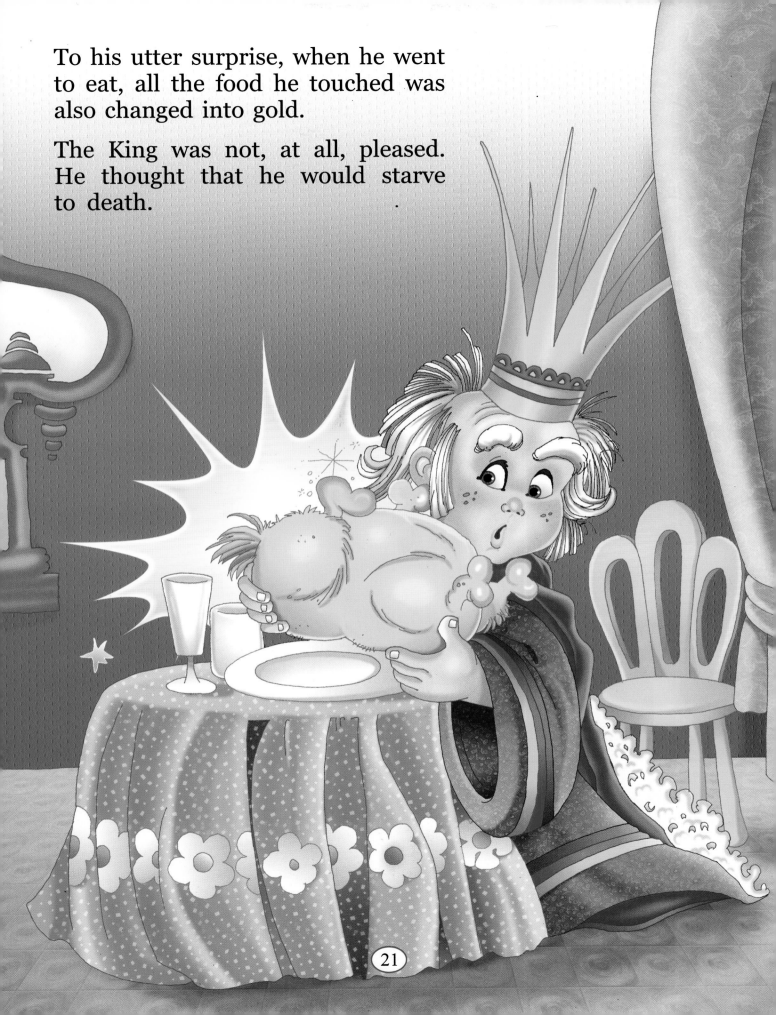

The next day, the Princess came to the King to give him a kiss. Lo and behold ! she too was changed into gold.

'What a dreadful thing !' the King cried.

22

The King called upon the magician again and asked him, "Please rid me of my magic touch. My darling daughter has turned into a gold statue and I have not eaten for three days. Please turn my daughter back into a real maiden. She is worth more to me than all my treasure."

The magician waved his magic wand and turned everything back to its original state.

King Midas understood that gold does not bring happiness. He distributed his treasures among the poor.

LITTLE RED RIDING HOOD

Little Red Riding Hood was a very pretty girl. She wore a red hood that her grandmother had given her.

Her grandmother lived by herself in a house in the wood. One day, Little Red Riding hood's mother said to her, "Take this basket to your grandmother as she is ill. Do take care not to talk to any stranger on the way."

Little Red Riding Hood had hardly covered a little distance when she met a wolf. The wolf said to her, "Where are you going ?"

"I am taking this basket to my grandmother who is ill," said Little Red Riding Hood.

The wolf suggested that they should play a game. He said to her, "Let us see who gets to your grandmother's house first. You can take the short cut; I shall stay on the path." Little Red Riding Hood agreed to what the wolf had said. The intentions of the wolf were not good. He had sent the little girl by the longest route because he himself wanted to get there first.

When the wolf arrived at the grandmother's house, he knocked at the door. "Who is it ?" asked the old lady.

"It is I, Little Red Riding Hood," said the wolf by changing his voice.

"Come in, dear; the door is open," said the old lady.

The wolf locked up the old lady in a cupboard, put on her clothes and got into her bed.

A moment later, Little Red Riding Hood arrived. "Oh Grandma ! what big eyes you have !" said the little girl.

"I see you with these eyes, my dear," said the disguised wolf.

"What big teeth you have !" said the little girl.

"I eat you with these teeth," said the wolf.

Saying so, the wolf pounced upon the poor little girl. She screamed, "Help ! Help !"